Unlucky Lucky Days

Unlucky Lucky Days

Stories by

Daniel Grandbois

AMERICAN READER SERIES, NO. 9

BOA EDITIONS, LTD. ❧ ROCHESTER, NY ❧ 2008

08 09 10 11   7 6 5 4 3 2

For information about permission to reuse any material from this book please
contact The Permissions Company at www.permissionscompany.com or e-mail
permdude@eclipse.net.

Publications and programs by BOA Editions, Ltd.—a not-for-profit
corporation under section 501 (c) (3) of the United States Internal
Revenue Code—are made possible with the assistance of grants from
the Literature Program of the New York State Council on the Arts; the
Literature Program of the National Endowment for the Arts; the County
of Monroe, NY; the Lannan Foundation for support of the Lannan Translations
Selection Series; the Sonia Raiziss Giop Charitable Foundation; the
Mary S. Mulligan Charitable Trust; the Rochester Area Community
Foundation; the Arts & Cultural Council for Greater Rochester; the
Steeple-Jack Fund; the Ames-Amzalak Memorial Trust in memory of
Henry Ames, Semon Amzalak and Dan Amzalak; and contributions from
many individuals nationwide.

See Colophon on page 126 for special individual acknowledgments.

Cover Design: Steve Smock
Cover Photograph: Gary Isaacs
Interior Design and Composition: Richard Foerster
Manufacturing: Thomson-Shore
BOA Logo: Mirko

Library of Congress Cataloging-in-Publication Data

Grandbois, Daniel.
  Unlucky lucky days : fictions / by Daniel Grandbois. — 1st ed.
      p. cm. — (American reader's series ; no. 9)
  ISBN 978–1–934414–10–1 (pbk. : alk. paper)
  I. Title.
PS3607.R36268U55 2008
813'.6—dc22
                            2007038076

BOA Editions, Ltd.
Nora A. Jones, Executive Director/Publisher
Thom Ward, Editor/Production
Peter Conners, Editor/Marketing
Glenn William, BOA Board Chair
A. Poulin, Jr., Founder (1938–1996)
250 North Goodman Street, Suite 306
Rochester, NY 14607
www.boaeditions.org

NATIONAL
ENDOWMENT
FOR THE ARTS

State of the Arts

NYSCA

For Irene Vilar

DAYS

⇒ SUNDAY ⇐

⇒ MONDAY ⇐

⇛ TUESDAY ⇚

⇛ WEDNESDAY ⇚

⇒ Saturday ⇐

⇒⇐

Unlucky Lucky Days

Sunday

THE YARN

A skein of yarn was unwound and wound in the shy hours before dawn. Yarn is naturally nocturnal and achieves locomotion by unwinding and then winding. This particular purple skein would have been fifty yards end to end, had a bramble not caught and kept a long piece of its tail months before. Undomesticated yarn can live up to a year.

Frayed by so many grabbing hands (the rough textures it passed over), the aging yarn pulled itself along, searching for nothing in particular, as that is what yarns do, except the call of almost anyone at all.

"Tell us your tale," a violin spider obliged from its loosely woven web.

The yarn stopped in its tracks and laid itself out, as that is how yarns tell their tales.

"Leaves one unsatisfied," commented the spider. "The ending is too abrupt."

MIGRATION

The road is littered with those who didn't make it. When the litter encroaches our encampments, we clear it. Sometimes with shovels. Others with bulldozers.

We must have done something terribly wrong. That is why we dance.

A growing child on each hip and full baskets on head, the women carry our burden down paths of mud. Men choose instead to kill and die among screeching birds, which are everywhere, always.

The migration took place over many lands.

Larry linked sausages together to keep us going.

We followed the water until it dried. Cursing, we debated going on. Turning back was worse. Six hundred felt otherwise. We didn't see them again until our return—their bones, a trail of breadcrumbs, leading us home.

THE GUM

Between this sentence and the last, an old crone chewed three wads of gum until each had lost its flavor. She spat them on the sidewalk into a less-than-perfect yet more-than-perfect triangle...

Between this sentence and the last, a baker lost her sense of smell. There was little difference anymore between the pastries and the pies, the baklava and the breads. She quit, though baking had been her ambition.

On the sidewalk before her were three wads of gum. The first spoke, as if to the others, "You see what ambition gets you."

"And working with baked goods," added the second.

"A jelly belly and day-old hopes," said the third...

Between this sentence and the last, three wads of gum appeared on the sidewalk, as if out of thin air.

"When shall we three meet again," said the first.

"When the hurly-burly's done," replied the second.

The silence of the third spoke volumes to the others.

One by one they attached themselves to the shoes of passersby, thus beginning the next round of their metaphysical game.

By the time the wads met again in a garbage heap, the fortunes of the three ill-fated humans were stuck together...

Between this sentence and the last, a new constellation appeared. Not in the sky, of course, for groupings of stars are not born all at once, but on the sidewalk, where anything is possible. After much debate over angles, the constellation of gum wads was named Pythagoras.

THE STAIN

To the left of the wolf spider was a stain on the cement floor. The shape of the stain suggested it had more abdomens than the spider but no legs. To the spider's right was a section of newspaper from another time. To the right of that, a wall. Beyond the wall, a stairway. Up the stairway went the stain. It had legs after all—abdomen-shaped to be sure—though not as many as the spider. It hobbled on three like a wounded dog.

On gaining the landing, the stain quickly pressed itself against the floor until three pairs of shod feet passed by and the flooring stopped shaking.

The world was different from the one the stain had known. It could tell immediately by the casual shoes and pant-legs. Its older twin had been born on a more meaningful pair of pants a hair's breadth in time before this one came to life on the cement. Soon after, there was water running upstairs, and its brother was gone.

Stains are usually reluctant to move. They must be pushed along—and forcefully—which usually ends badly, at least for the stain. What made this one move of its own will after eighty-six years? It loathed the idea of carpet. Some sandals and denim pants had already come to measure the room. The basement was being finished.

Happy Birthday Grandma

She was a giraffe of modest proportions, except for her spots, which threatened to overtake her. Her white socks had escaped the spots by threatening, in turn, to pull themselves up. They were knee-highs already, and her knees were each as high as a pyramid of squirrel monkeys. Her front knees bent one way and her back knees bent the other, so, by bringing her hooves together, she was able to make a sweet circle of her legs and underbelly, the hairs of which were in league with the socks. The giraffe usually performed this maneuver just before lying down. If she wasn't careful about it, she squeezed Mrs. Humperdink Hedgehog, who liked to curl into a ball and roll herself through the circle at the last moment. Well, if Mrs. Humperdink got squeezed, it certainly hurt the giraffe too, whose name, you shall now learn, was Happy Birthday Grandma, despite the fact that she wasn't anybody's mother. Happy Birthday's neck was said to grow an inch of a sudden every time she caught Mrs. Humperdink in her circle. Still, you couldn't stop the hedgehog from risking her life, though she had seven children to think about and a block of wood she liked to call her eighth. Anyway, this is the story of how birthdays got started and Happy got her name.

Once upon a time, nobody was born. Obviously, then, no one had even heard of a birthday, much less a happy one, and they hadn't the faintest idea what a grandma was, unless it was the sound you made when you tasted something sour.

There isn't much to live for when you were never born, at least that's what these things thought at the time, not that time was a thing itself just yet, as time also has something to do with birth. So the unborn things hatched a plan for some birthing to begin.

They felt around for a stick and stuck it in the ground. Then, they waited for lightning to strike it. Lightning was new then and seemed to be changing things for the better. Still, the thunderclaps scared the living daylights out of these creatures who didn't even know what daylight was.

The waiting was easy. Such beings could wait forever. They weren't going anywhere. Eventually, lightning struck and caught the stick on fire. The creatures scattered in fear. Once they returned, they had no idea what to do next. This had been the extent of their plan—to stick something in the ground and wait for lightning. These weren't the brightest things ever to *not* live. To be fair, it would have been hard for anyone to be bright in all that darkness. That was one of the things lightning was changing for the better—how often you could see things. You'd get a flash now and then and know you were in Cleveland, or something like that.

Anyway, the flaming stick gave a spooky glow to their faces before burning itself to the ground. The feeling was sweet, however bitter, and that was the first sweetness there was.

It was also the first deathday, as the stick was gone. Needless to say, the first birthday followed shortly thereafter. They celebrated the occasion with their happy instrument of death, namely the flaming stick, and also with the clapping of thunder.

What was born, grew, somewhat from the ashes of the two burned sticks that, for some reason, had not blown away. Nobody is sure what wind was like then.

The creatures gathered and did their magic until the ground was covered in ashes and also with the new things that were being born. Each of them had a birthday, which included a deathday as before, so after each birthday, even more things were born. It was a circle.

About that time, for time was now rolling, something startling happened. A new thing was born from something already born—in other words, motherhood began. And that first little being born of the first mother cried in such distress that it blew its burning stick right out.

You will have guessed that this soon became part of the ceremony. At least when mothers were the cause of the birth, which they became more and more. After that, there was great hoopla in the thunderstorms as each new thing was born, and then everyone shouted, "Blow out your stick!"

But they couldn't hear each other over all that thunder. Besides, they were growing tired of having to wait forever for lightning to strike a stick to begin their birthday parties. It was decided that fire should be caught and kept on hand. Also, they would replace the thunderclaps with clapping of their own. No one knew how to do that yet, so they practiced with only one hand at first, until they got good enough to use both.

And, of course, the birthdays piled up, so more sticks were added, and mothers became grandmothers, because there was just no avoiding it.

After a long while, there was such a thing as a grandmother giraffe—well, she wasn't a grandmother yet, but she wanted to be so badly. She wanted it more than anything else, even two new pairs of winter socks. Her birthday rolled around and, fortunately for us, she got her wish. Her very first grandbaby plopped out on the ground. Can you guess what those in attendance said? That's right. "Happy Birthday, Grandma!" So that became the baby's name, because giraffes had, by then, already begun their tradition of naming their children with the first words uttered by anyone at the birth.

This explains why giraffes have such names as "Eww Gross" and "Stop Licking Your Nose!" Happy Birthday Grandma considered herself lucky.

Her luck was about to run out. Just as our tale was winding down—I hope we didn't distract the giraffe with such a ridiculous story—Mrs. Humperdink Hedgehog pulled one of her stunts and got herself caught in Happy Birthday's circle. She was crushed to death. "My poor block of wood!" was the last thing she said.

Happy Birthday Grandma went on living for several more days. The spines in her white belly made that part of her look like an upside-down birthday cake. It proved to be a deathday cake instead, as her injuries overtook her—socks, spots and all. Lying on the hard ground beside a heap of sticks, she said, "What a bitter-sweet circle you turned out to be." She hadn't lived long enough to become a mother, much less a *grand* one.

THE URGE

Forty days and nights later, the urge left the clouds. It landed on a stone, which was grateful, as it had never had much of an urge to do anything.

Now the stone felt it could explode and didn't mind the thought. Even the aftermath of living as many pieces seemed appealing: what perspective could be gained!

Still, it only lay there.

"Where did this urge come from, anyway?" the stone tortured itself in philosophical moments. "I never had an urge before. Why now? Why this?"

But the stone had misinterpreted the urge, which was spent after its time in the clouds. The urge had only come to rest where it thought it would be safe from the delusions of a god.

THE PRAYER

Still held in place by ligaments, the skeletons of former chiefs were wrapped in their own cleaned and treated skins, once the muscle had been scraped off.

Ten skin-and-bones chiefs lay in wait, side by side, on a platform high enough to foil other predators, while children played and spooked themselves near it.

Beneath the chiefs, some of whose stitched skins were older than the living, a pelt was spread out in the dirt. Crawling over this, the shaman shook his rattles.

On closer examination, the hairs of the pelt were tall buildings with broken windows and people inside.

THE FISH

A dried fish stood in a glass case on the table like an auto-graphed baseball. It wore earrings and spoke through a tube. Its voice crackled on like a loudspeaker at a grocery, the words sometimes discernible but usually not.

The fish had arrived suddenly from elsewhere and quickly earned its position on the table. We wanted to touch it, to smell it and put it in our mouths. Yet, we were also frightened and repulsed.

Though it appeared to breathe, it did not. At least not according to our instruments, which were the only thing it let near enough to tell. We measured everything about it and still we knew nothing. How did it get here? From where? What was it saying and why?

Over time, we got used to it. We returned to our tasks and forgot about the fish.

THE GROWTH

They toasted good health without looking at the growth on Aunt Mary. The growth wondered what it would be like to hold a hand in the air and clink glasses. Seen at certain wavelengths, the growth had hands of its own, buzzing around its mass like a magnetic field. But they lacked a certain freedom. Fantasizing again, the growth imagined its hands dribbling its body like a basketball, up and down the long table, and then diving through the air into Aunt Mary's glass. That would really make a splash. Or, what if it could attach itself to Todd? Everyone was always looking at Todd and asking him to speak. How had it ended up on Aunt Mary anyway—and her neck? It seemed as random as the decay of an isotope in an old growth forest when no one is there to hear.

THE LOG

Once upon a log, a human face was carved. All the more striking as it was carved by a chimp. He'd meant to carve his own face, but his use of tools was limited. Plus, accidents will happen, most always leading to things breaking. That was the chimp's experience, anyway. Just look at how the protruding snout broke off here. And the prominent brow ridge, which was still in his hand.

The chimpanzee buried the brow ridge in a termite mound where he had gone to look for food, but what interests us now is the log, which was not pleased.

It barked, "Don't stop at the face, Panzee! Cut some fists and let's see if you can take it like a man!"

Monday

THE TERMITE QUEEN

All was as it should be for the termite Queen. The blind Soldiers were stopping up passages from intrusion with their heads. The blind Workers were tunneling, foraging, collecting, storing, digesting for the others and feeding them from their anuses. Her little King was nearby and ever ready, and she had succeeded in increasing her size 100,000% by growing an additional set of ovaries with each molt. So, why was she unhappy when hundreds of Workers moved her? Or when they lapped up the reward she secreted?

There was her body, and then there was she. She didn't want to distend her abdomen any further. She didn't want to lay another thousand eggs. She was tired of being fed by the Workers. Yet, such things just kept happening. She might as well have been a side effect for all she seemed to matter.

Thinking these thoughts, the Queen was pushed into a deeper chamber. Another intrusion of ants. When one tunnel-blocking Soldier went down, another took its place. They banded together in the wider breaches, biting with their huge jaws and squirting toxic glue from their noses, while behind them Workers repaired the breaches. This had the regrettable effect of sealing the Soldiers out. And still the ants got through.

STILL LIFE WITH PAINTER

The painter did not move. His assistants moved things around him. Now, he was in the kitchen. Now, in his bed. The fruit bowl was brought to his face so he could eat avocados and pomegranates by using only his jaw. The carafe was drunk from similarly, as well as the porcelain teacup and the indelicate glass of wine. Once a day, a bouquet of flowers was put beneath his nose for sniffing, which he did without a sound.

They touched canvases to his brush. This was the most demanding task, not for the obvious reasons but because his long, curling fingernails had never been cut.

In the master's most revealing self-portrait, everything is moving. The golden hair wilts like a sunflower. The throat bobs like an apple. And the hands claw at the canvas to get to the man.

ORANGUTAN

They were definitely orangutan hairs, sprouting from his forehead. His genealogy revealed nothing, unless the eighth son of a potato farmer had dabbled abroad in his prodigal half year.

At the Cincinnati Zoo, the man plucked the hairs by the root and blew them into the orangutan exhibit, on loan from Pittsburgh. They settled on an orange rind.

The man's throat began to swell and his body to itch.

In sniffing the rind, an orangutan inhaled the hairs but not before the man had tossed in his hat. The ape was about to fill the hat with feces when a thought occurred to him, and he filled it instead with his hair.

TOOTHPASTE

From the moment I recognized it was Carl's teeth banging around in the dryer, I went deaf. I popped open the metal door, and the little, yellowed cubes rained down, skipping or sliding to rest, but the sound was white as cotton and five times as dense.

I found Carl in the kitchen. His toothbrush and a bloody pair of pliers on the counter. He was trying to tell me something. Not knowing I'd gone deaf, he got furious and grabbed the pliers.

In the basement, beside the dryer, he was jamming the last molar back into his mouth.

The pliers hit the cement floor with a clunk. I could hear again. Carl hollered, "We're out of toothpaste!"

THE SOUND

There once was a sound that made a nest of the hairs in some woman's ear. Given that it was the first such nest this sound ever made, it wasn't quite sure if it would remain a sound when it settled down or transform into some butterfly. This was one of the things it wanted to find out. The others had to do with body memory and a certain theory of space that made it possible for two things to occupy the same nest at once, as long as they behaved less like particles than waves. Unsure it could behave like a particle if it wanted to, the sound settled into the nest and called for a mate. But, apparently, it could no longer be heard. Believing it had become inaudible, the sound snuck down the ear canal for some Peeping Tom-ery and found out immediately how mistaken it was. The woman shrieked at the voice in her head.

THE NOTE

A note was pinned to a man in his coffin. It said, "I only seem dead." The man's sister had pinned it there, as she'd pinned it to his pajamas before bed each night—so afraid was he of being buried alive.

With her help, he'd escaped that dreadful fate.

She, however, did not.

Staring up at her own coffin lid, his sister wished he'd stayed around a bit longer to pin the note to her.

But they'd had more dirt between them than this. She reached over, removed the note from his chest and pinned it to her blouse.

She died, smiling wryly.

As for the note, in whichever coffin it now rests, it had never pretended to speak for anyone but itself.

CORE TRUTHS

An apple core was lying awake, which was unusual because most of the time it did its lying in its sleep. It tossed and turned and lost a seed, one of a half dozen black hearts that dreamed of harder skin.

Much as a stone takes to it, the seed took to lying. It had not fallen far from the core. But the core had fallen far from the tree. Or, rather, it'd been taken away after falling, though, it must be said, it was an apple then.

A woman had eaten of the wrinkly-skinned fruit. She'd done so specifically because it was fermented. Over the years, her root cellar became home to many cores, but no seed ever took. Much as a Swedish moose, the wrong-headed woman walked farther and farther out onto the ice.

THE MIRROR

I was pulled from the nothing that connects all reflective surfaces. Since then, I've had a place in the world, a point of view. Currently, it's from the south wall in the entryway of this house on Amherst Circle. I've had others, as well as glimpses through mirrors in dreams.

I've seen humans grow from babies twenty-three times. They keep one foot in my world for about two years. After that, they see only their own reflections. Except Louie.

I've always read books over people's shoulders, even back in the farmhouse. One of your writers describes being born as having your peephole opened to the world. I think he got it right. That's exactly how it felt when my tin was pressed to glass. Since then, like you, I've been doing my best not to fall.

Something from the maple tree came into me when I got my frame, a more hurried sense of time than glass or tin has, yet far less hurried than man's. But my perceptions were so new, it was hard to tell what was what, what was where, and what was when. I heard what I would call stones today and imagined they were rumblings from one of Jupiter's moons, none of which were known to have active volcanoes at the time, so it couldn't have been a projection, though mirrors, I can now admit, are great projectors.

Louie's peephole was opened the same day as mine in the farmhouse. He got all the attention, but I understand. Your kind needs it to keep your peepholes from closing. Though he lived to fifty-eight, he kept a foot in my world.

Mirrors slip in and out of dreams. That's the only way I can explain where I was. Torches made shadows bob about the cavern like puppets, while three figures, who'd been waiting in the antechamber, now gazed into the mirrorlike water. The first became a winking eye; the second a black dog to guard it; the third a ropelike snake by which men might reach it. They withdrew to some other plane, leaving only the bobbing shadows. When the flames went out, I woke to Louie's body on the bed.

THE WIFE

These lines, these folds, this frog's-leg thumb, these bumps, these pads, these elephant-knee knuckles, this callus, this yielding to pressure, this salamander wrist, these goose-skin pores and earthworm veins—like the pine of the same age out front, you've grown into this hand.

Except for the hand, her body was on her side of the bed, supported by failing pillows. She'd left the door open, ostensibly for air, but her eyes remained fixed on what was stuck to the window—a blankness to swim your head through.

She said, "I grew into your wife."

CROQUET

In a pile of dead, one was living. He made an igloo of the corpses, which didn't stink in the cold. Instead of animal hides, his bedclothes were their clothes, sewn into blankets. These did smell, especially after a winter in them.

With the thaw, the roof began to leak. It leaked until it caved in. Then, the bears came, attracted by the smell.

When the bears died, their corpses froze into a constellation of arches. We use them today for whacking colored balls of children through on their way to the North Pole, which is wooden and striped like a rainbow.

THE BREAST

A man floated into the room, his hand glued to his wife's breast. Another man with scissors cut him out of the air and put the cutout on the sofa where it belonged. The wife lost her breast in the operation but carried on at the party as if she were whole. Because of where his hand was, the man still believed he was floating.

Tuesday

SVEVO

He trotted out a horse he'd made of clay and painted yellow in his youth. I asked to touch it. He put it away. Both ears had broken off already.

He placed in my hands a house he'd made of Popsicle sticks and decorated with patterned fabric and lace.

Inside, a pair of hairy horse ears twitched and turned.

Jumping the box, they listened at his bedroom door, sticking to it like thick-bodied spiders. He pried and pulled, but they burrowed into the wood until only the hairs were left. He shaved them off.

But he couldn't sleep with the ears in his door. I held a match to the ovals of darkened wood. They came backing out, shriveled in the flames and dropped to the floor.

Retrieving his clay horse, Svevo glued on its ears.

"Every seventeen years," he said. "Like locusts."

THE LAST COWBOY

Bill was the last cowboy in the Eskimo village. He'd been the first one too, and they weren't going to be looking for any more.

"Why do cowboys always do this kind of shit?" was a common lament in their igloos, even though none of them had had any experience with cowboys before. Still, they could just tell that cowboys must always do this kind of shit because Bill was so good at it.

The men fashioned a special meeting-lodge igloo and held a meeting about it.

"Goddamn it!" said one Eskimo.

"Right!" said another.

"Shit!" said a third.

"Goddamn," echoed the youngest.

"I think we covered that," said his father.

"He said, 'Goddamn *it*,'" the youth chafed. "I said Goddamn."

"This is his doing," said another, speaking of the cowboy. "He's turned man against father."

The meeting didn't resolve much so they decided to have a spirit lodge.

The Great Spirit advised them: "The cowboy must go."

"But he married my daughter," said an elder.

"Hmmm," said the Great Spirit. "That does present a problem."

The men nodded.

The air spoke again: "The daughter must go, too."

All but one of them grunted assent. The same elder as before only rubbed his bald chin. "But she is the mother of my grandchildren."

"Why didn't you say this before?" the Great Spirit coughed in anger. This put out the small fire the men had built in order to see their maker, who was invisible, except for his shadow. Now, it was all shadow in there, and each of them was afraid he was being taken to the Great Shadow behind the moon.

Bill's father-in-law was the most frightened of all. He'd laid the cowboy trap in the first place, using his daughter as bait.

The Great Spirit spoke: "The grandchildren must go."

Much relieved, the men clapped, "Hey! Hey!"

The father-in-law snuck out. He rounded up his family in the dark and made them walk north to where the snow never melted. Saving the cowboy suit for his grandson, he laid a trap for a goddamn rodeo clown.

THE NEWSPAPER

Having been read only once, the usual story, the small-town newspaper was stuffed in a cereal box, slated for the can. It tried to strike up a conversation, but the box couldn't read, no matter the words splattered over it.

Ah, but, miracle of miracles, the paper was retrieved. It shouted for joy, something it very rarely did, which sounded like this: !. But then the newspaper was separated into three pages and folded and creased in unnatural places.

It became a hat, an airplane, and a sailboat.

"Look at me," said the hat, perched high on the bald man's head, greedily soaking up the sweat.

"What about meeeeeeeeeeee?" asked the airplane, soaring through the dining room. It had borrowed several *e*'s from different places to ask such a question, as no respectable paper was going to print more than two in a row. With an anticlimactic crinkle, the airplane crashed to the floor.

For no apparent reason, the plane and hat were gathered and lit on fire.

Carrying the news, the boat set sail down a gutter but took on too much water and was soon despondent in the sewer, where the rats, to its horror, could read.

THE MANSION

There once was an executioner in retirement. A large turtle he was and happy to have finally moved from town to the country. He hated town, but more than that, he hated mansions. Imagine his dismay then when he came across a mansion on his afternoon walk by the creek.

The odd thing about this mansion was its size. It was very small, which upset the turtle no end. Bad enough to find a mansion by the creek on your afternoon walk, but a miniature mansion? It mocked him. He must come out of retirement at once and execute it.

You see, this turtle had not been an executioner of the kinds of things you might expect, like No-Goodsies and Enemies of the Town. He executed powdered wigs, dictionaries, and structures that were too big.

He sent word to the new mayor, asking for assistance, and returned one day from his walk to find an ugly chair on the porch. Not at all the kind you might rock in. He was about to get angry when he opened the manual and discovered the chair was a newfangled execution device. The turtle fetched the mansion at once.

Having placed it on the chair, he attached the wires as the manual prescribed. Then, he threw the switch. Lights flew on, and a churning noise came from something in the kitchen that the old turtle couldn't know was a dishwasher. The electric chair only made the mansion more alive!

Much as he hated to, the turtle would have to go to town. He'd tell that upstart mayor what he thought of his chair. Then, he'd arrange for his friends, the woodworker and the blacksmith, to build him an old-fashioned guillotine.

They'd do the job as it should be done, no matter the years heaped on their shells.

The mayor refused to see him, of course, so he and his friends gathered at the blacksmith's house. Over soup, the turtle appealed to their pride, asking them to fashion a guillotine as only such masters could. He told them it was to execute a mansion he'd been unlucky enough to find by the creek. Worked up as he was, he forgot to mention that this particular mansion was actually quite small.

As he was leaving, he asked the blacksmith if he could still sharpen a blade.

"Of course I can!" growled the blacksmith, but, because his eyesight was fading, he said it to the woodworker.

Finally, the agreed-upon day arrived.

"Dead mansion walking," the turtle joked as he carried the mansion to town.

In the public square, the guillotine was ready, but the turtle couldn't see it. The woodworker pointed proudly overhead. As you will have guessed, the guillotine had been built to execute a less modest mansion.

"Decrepit old hardshells!" the turtle snapped. "*This* is the mansion!" He held it before them. Setting it down, he made a show of stepping over it twice. "Do you see? Do you *see*?" The blade above them did not glint in the bright morning light. "I can see from here, it's as flat as your head!" he shouted at the blacksmith. "How can I execute a mansion with that spatula? It would only be smashed to bits."

Upset, the blacksmith stumbled away and bumped into one of the structure's legs. The whole thing began to moan. Of a sudden, the blade came down. The executioner only had time to retreat into his shell.

He was squashed to just the right size to fit nicely in the mansion, which sat beside him, untouched.

The mayor came out of his office at once and offered grandly to place the mansion with the turtle inside on a pedestal in the square as a sort-of monument to something or other.

"He hated that mansion," protested the woodworker.

"I could use a paperweight," the town librarian declared, and that's where you can find the executioner right down to this day—in the fish tank near the children's books at the Boulder Public Library.

THE HORSE

A husband and wife fell off a horse and refused to climb back on. The husband cited the horse's sagging back; the wife, its short fuse. The husband called the horse a cow; the wife, a jackass. The husband threatened to whip it; the wife, to ignore it. Meanwhile, the horse was having its day. One after the other, it kicked them through manure and dried-out fields, where weed stalks and feathers stuck to them. Then, it kicked them back across the country road, up the marble steps and through the oaken doors of their elegant, rented villa.

COUNTER-PUNCHER

He was a natural counter-puncher, so it was a shame nobody
would attack. Tired of waiting, his fists turned on him. He
countered with his feet, but his eyes were with his hands.
They helped his hands find his face and land with preci-
sion. That is, until the blows swelled them shut. After that,
his hands moved in the same darkness as his feet and every
other part of him.

But soon he saw he could feel what he could no longer
see. He felt his fists, measuring him out. He felt the presence
of others, including his dead mother and the cat in her lap.
He felt the slipping of his once tight grip. Then, he felt a
blow he could never have seen coming and saw pinholes of
light, as if through a mask.

A Bicycle Built for Two

It was a bicycle built for two, but only one was left to ride it. The other, Harry's twin goat, had stopped one day at a mulberry bush and now couldn't stop going around it.

Harry had the rear seat redone in cowhide in memory of his brother, or his brother's behind, depending on how you looked at it. He tried to ride it from there but always fell over. Once, he scraped his own hide nearly through to his breakfast.

What else could one do with a bicycle built for two?

"I'll sell it!" Harry bleated, but no one would buy it.

So, Harry made wings of straw and stuck them into the pedals. His plan was to fly over the bush until his brother looked up, at which point, he'd swoop down and swing him onto the back.

But it was not to be. Though Harry pedaled furiously, the bike only lifted high enough to knock his brother into the bush. And Harry went crashing over it to his death.

The bicycle's remains were laid in the casket with Harry. Chomping mulberry leaves, his brother looked on, wearing the chain loosely around his neck like a rapper.

NEWSHOUND

The anchor turns from profile. The long nose sweeps the air, its hair neatly clipped. But there's a pause. The anchor appears to examine a plant hanging above the stage manager's desk in the distance.

The anchor is fifty-five. He has the habit of playing with his nose. He bends it to the left and to the right. He runs his fingers down its flanks. With his thumb and forefinger, he enters the nostrils together and massages the septum, sometimes squeezing it to flatten the bulge it has made to the right since a drill instructor in basic training knocked him unconscious. The anchor must keep an eye on his fingers, as the public's eye is ever on him.

His sense of smell is not what it used to be. There was a time in his youth when he could name the plant he was approaching before he could see it, distinguishing, for example, the rainy musk of creosote through a foreground of wet asphalt.

He has added a new element to his routine before bed. After flossing, brushing, and washing his face, he picks.

"I can't breathe!" he snaps when his wife, without allowing herself to look at him, demands to know what he's doing.

Receiving his cue, the anchor removes a pine needle from his suit pocket and holds it to the camera without saying a word.

THE TUNNEL

A man and a woman stepped into a tunnel. It was lighter inside than they had expected. In fact, the deeper they went, the lighter it became until the light was so bright that it blinded them both.

SNOWMEN

Over the course of a snowman's life, there are three hurdles he must clear. The first being keeping himself together. Second, and a big part of the first, is learning to stay cool. In order to do that, the snowman must spring over the third hurdle first—learning to turn the heat of others back onto them, like a jujitsu master.

A snowman uses his senses to aid him. The crooked carrot sniffs out danger, as well as sharpening the eyesight. The eyes of coal let him see quickly into black hearts. The broccoli stumps, if they haven't been cropped too closely, enable him to hear branching trees falling in faraway forests, though, admittedly they're deaf as cauliflower at close range. And the smoking of the corncob pipe not only gives the snowman a tactile sense of his enemy, heat, but also the distinct privilege of tasting it.

Once these hurdles have been negotiated successfully, the accomplished snowman may wish to gather his balls and tumble out of there, but first he must ask himself, "Where in hell would I go?"

THE WARMTH

I'm in my bag all the time now. To venture out is to risk becoming part of the landscape—at least until the thaw, if there's ever going to be one. The landscape was liquid once, as far as the tentacle could feel. We soaked in it, day and night. Hank's dendritic limbs touched mine. Mine touched Susan's and Sarah's. We passed sacks of sugar back and forth.

Sean invented the mummy-bags, but they can't hold the warmth. Judy taught us to sheathe our skin in strips of mucus-soaked cloth to no avail. Previously, we'd known it only from stories around the fire: when the warmth is done, it moves on.

Soon, we change our blood for antifreeze. At least our bodies will be preserved for the next go around.

Wednesday

THREE WISE MEN

On a mountaintop a foot wide, three wise men made their perch. Each had to sit on the lap of the next. They took turns at the bottom of the top, the middle of the top and the top of the top, trading places every fortnight.

In the village below, this rotation was called The Re-ordering of the Wise and was celebrated with roast pig, followed by three hours of fasting, one for each wise man, while the pig meat was digested.

Once, a small boy ascended the mountain. He fell to his death a quarter way up. Neither his journey nor his death was celebrated by anyone, except the three wise men, who concealed their joy somewhere in their eyes. When a wise man's eyes began to buzz like a No Vacancy sign, he was taken down from the mountain and made to walk through the village wearing sunglasses and a dunce cap.

In celebrating their good fortune, the two remaining wise men would come that much closer to being removed themselves.

The women in the village did the removing. Surprisingly, they had little trouble going up and down the mountain when it was needed of them. And they had little trouble finding another man to sit up there in the cold.

THE HERMIT CRAB

There once was a hermit crab who lived by the sea, all alone in the sand, except for his nineteen brothers and sisters who always got in the way, sixteen of which were not even related to him and had no business going about where he was.

Oh, how he wished his siblings knew better how to live up to their name. "We're *hermit* crabs," he used to tell them. "*Hermit, hermit, hermit!* Don't any of you get it?"

"A hermit lives alone," they said, "not in a pile of others. A hermit has long hair, whereas we have none. A hermit is not what we are," they said emphatically, "and not at all what we've already named ourselves, which you should know by now fits like a shell. That is, Not-Lobster-Not-Crawfish-Not-Oyster-Not-Shrimp."

"Yes, I know," said the crab before saying nothing to them ever again. "We named ourselves after the things we are not. Well, then, if we're not hermits, as you say, *Hermit Crabs* should suit you fine."

To this quip, his nineteen brothers and sisters gave no answer, except to crawl all over each other into a pyramid-shaped pile that pointed at a passing cloud, until the top-most crab tumbled off and, shame-faced, retracted into his shell. He was the heaviest and should have known to stay at the bottom.

So, our hermit crab packed up his shell with his few belongings, which consisted of a pebble, and moved to Salt Lake City, where, at least, nobody would know him. If he kept to himself, it might stay that way, too. Then, they'd all know who was right about their name.

ALMOST BORGES

The old man made a list of things that would not notice his death. Pocket change. *Leaves of Grass.* Deck of cards. Somewhere in the middle, he put down the pen, took off his glasses and rubbed the bone around his eyes.

Then, his knuckled hand left him for a cold cup of tea.

Meanwhile, the arm of his chair supported a stiff cane that was unquestionably on its last leg. Elsewhere in the house, a hot-water bottle was blobbing its way across the bathroom floor, trying to relieve itself so it could travel lighter. And a thermometer, believing its problems all imaginary, leapt from the medicine cabinet without a parachute. The mercury and hot water did not mix on the floor.

The teacup could not agree with the man's stroke-twisted lip and was returned to the saucer on his desk. At the man's insistence, the pen bled further onto the page. The blood spread through the paper. The paper floated into a drawer that, for the first time in all its hardwood years, would not close.

NEW HEAVEN

In the end, only three were saved from the heap. A fish, a fowl, and a fool. The fool had been taken from the equivalent of a high king's court; the others, from sea and sky. All such domains were part of the heap.

The one who saved? An insurance salesman from Buffalo.

The reason? None given.

Their new heaven? An unfinished basement, still flooded by record-setting rain.

Wearing chest waders, the salesman would visit them often, but only at night when they couldn't see him. His splashing and sloshing led them to imagine all manner of savior—from a fish to a fowl to a fool, respectively.

One night, the sloshing sounds were different. Having learned of what her husband had done, the salesman's wife thought she would take a turn. The waders were big on her, but the sounds she made in them were smaller. The fish circled her thighs. The fowl her floating breasts. The fool waited in the corner, cockscomb in hand.

THE TEACHER

"I'm done being a carpenter," said the blind cat to his mother.

"But you're such a very good one."

"Does a good one nail his tail to the roof?"

"But how will we pay for our mice? You can't hunt in your condition."

"I must go to town and strike a bargain," said the cat. "The only question is, what service can I offer?"

"You could trim some nice kitten's hedges."

"I should not be handling gardening shears, Mother."

"Clean her attic, empty her litter boxes."

"Mother, your lack of schooling makes it abundantly clear that I must take this up on my own."

The next morning, the blind cat went to town, losing his way only once. There, he met all manner of creatures. None, however, could think of a service they needed performed or had any interest in hunting mice for him.

The cat was about to lose hope when he bumped into a mouse who was blind as well.

"I do apologize," said the mouse, brushing himself off.

"Pardon me," said the cat, licking himself clean.

They introduced themselves by name only, assuming the rest would be evident to the other, but their senses of smell had suffered along with their eyesight—the cat's, because of a nail through the nose; the mouse's, for congenital reasons. Only one of the mouse's many siblings could smell worth a whiff.

Surprisingly, the mouse offered to help. "You can count on me," he squeaked, believing the cat to be an overgrown

School Mouse who'd lost his students on a field trip to town. "A service in return? I'll have none of it. You do enough for our community already."

This was certainly a good citizen, thought the cat. He'd entertained the notion before that he did enough already. He only wished his mother could have heard it.

The mouse rounded up what school children he could find, which turned out to be a couple of worms trying to sneak into the movies.

The cat devoured one at once.

"Not as toothsome as a mouse," he said, sucking his teeth.

Then and there, the blind mouse might have assessed the situation clearly. Instead, he opened wide, thinking the teacher was remarking on his well-cared-for teeth.

Next, the mouse brought the cat a dead vole that it took to be lazy.

Soon enough, there were no school children left. The mouse eagerly offered himself as a pupil. He'd always wanted to learn the alphabet.

But the cat was not such a pig as all that. He had standards, especially with his friends, and a stiff backbone, even if he could twist it into a knot. In parting thanks, he took the mouse's paw. The sudden recognition gave them both a start.

Pouncing too late to catch the fleeing mouse, the blind cat's mother shrieked at her son. "I knew I'd find you dilly-dallying, but with a mouse! While your own mother starves at home? What a disgrace!"

"Calm down, Mother," said the cat. "I've landed a job as a schoolteacher. If you would do me the favor of guiding me home, I'd be only too happy to teach you a lesson."

Escape Artist

He remembers when there was no need to escape, when money fell like ripe fruit from the limbs of his parents. Now, he had to earn it. Trying to escape that fact almost cost him his life, while ironically proving his existence. "I can escape anything but my need to escape; therefore, I am," or something like that. The proper formation of a thought often escaped him, not to mention the names of his children, where he'd put his keys, the way home from the mall and how to spell *Albuquerque*.

The great escape, namely death, was yet to come. It put the artist in a quandary, for escaping an escape was tantamount to failing that escape, which, in his line of work, could prove fatal. Yet, death was the very escape he'd be 'scaping.

He went for a walk to clear his head. Before him in the park, vines clung to an oak. Suddenly, a boy was clambering up, ripping vines away with his hands and feet. As the light changed, the boy disappeared near the top.

The escape artist dropped his black satchel and went up.

The satchel has since been through many hands and would be unrecognizable to the man. Having found its way back to the oak, it waits like a dumb dog.

THE CENTIPEDE

A centipede with high arches dreamed of becoming a butterfly. It hobbled up an old log on the outside edges of its feet and hid beneath some bark, except for its eyes.

Whenever a butterfly landed, the gigantic, blinking eyes on its still-beating wings liked to tell the centipede how it could make arch supports from dead plant matter, but the centipede refused to listen because it was supposed to be hidden. Also, it didn't trust those eyes to tell it anything, much less about feet.

The caterpillars had large, sightless eyes, too, to distract predators. Other than that, they were much like the centipede, except inside they had wings, waiting to come out, and outside, ten of their sixteen legs would pull in.

So, the centipede ate all the wings it could find, from transparent insect wings to the old feathers of birds. And, it gnawed off and swallowed all but six of its legs, which did wonders for its arch pain. Finally, the centipede wrapped itself in spider silk, not thinking of the spider.

When it woke, it could fly like a butterfly but could no longer be seen.

HOME

The drapery didn't mind that its two halves might as well have been sewn together. Even so, thoughts of what it was hiding haunted the twelve-foot panels of blue velvet.

The window couldn't offer any help. It could see out, but it couldn't see in. Some days, it wished it were a mirror, not knowing that while it slept that's exactly what it was.

Sunny Side Up

She was a canary named Sunny Side Up. It was odd because her sunny side was down. The only yellow she'd hatched with was a circular patch underneath. And she'd developed the habit of hanging her head to try to see it, which made her name even more inappropriate.

Did I mention how little she sang? Oh, she sang when she bathed in the aqueducts, as long as no one was near, and she sang way up high in the coal-colored sky—swimming and diving, flitting and rising—but she wouldn't put two notes together to save her black throat if she thought any of the others could hear.

All their songs were just boasting anyway. Or, they sang so sincerely about mating for life. Their favorite song drove Sunny simply batty. It went on and on about the sunny side and how one should keep on it. It was just so inappropriate because all of them were caged.

Sunny Side Up was the last free canary. She lived alone in a small circle of wilderness, five feet wide. Sharing the wild with her was a juniper bush that was presently dying of freedom. It hadn't rained in months, and the bush couldn't fly to the aqueducts to sneak a drink. Also, sunlight no longer got through to it. Sunny tried to keep the juniper's spirits up by twittering on about rolling stones.

Don't jump to conclusions. Cages don't always mean humans, especially in stories in which there are none. Species of all kinds are more than happy to cage themselves. Then, their songs grow louder, the notes more shrill as they trill almost continuously from first light to bright night about their magnificent cages and all they contain—like feeding tubes and bird baths with ten kinds of shampoo.

The Ever After

At the end of the line stood a man most noted for the way he started things. It was he who began the middle of the bridge which led to the beginning of the end for those on the other side, none of whom were known for their beginnings or their endings, though their fat middles came to inhabit the rear ends of many jokes.

This was how it was. The line moved slowly. No one arrived to become the new end, so the man noted for his beginnings had to learn a few things about endings, most of which started something like this: all has been said or done; nothing left but the ever after.

Once whoever stood at the front removed him- or herself from the procession, the business at hand being completed to some degree or other of satisfaction, he or she went off in some direction that could be shown to be random if you studied the whole group.

Now was the man's turn.

And now the ever after.

Thursday

No Place to Crawl

I've wanted to tell you where we come from. When I was born, there was no place to lie down, much less to sit upon or crawl across. Every place was a place to fall, or so it seemed because of the way it felt, and sounded and looked, which was like nothing, nothing and nothing—in that order.

I couldn't see my seven toes wiggle or hear my five noses crack when I bent them to the side. Can you believe that? But I could talk in a silent kind of way that made my eyebrow skunch. At least I think it did. What few mirrors there might have been were impossible to see, though some of us now believe such infinite darkness had been a trick of theirs. Beware of mirrors.

So, I asked the emu, "Where is this world I'm supposed to roam?" and the emu said, "Boom!" which made things sound a little less like silence.

I asked the duck, "Where is this water I'm supposed to wade through?" and the duck said, "Goose!" Even then, ducks were good at playing games.

I asked the penguin, "Where is this ice I'm supposed to slip-slide on?" The penguin was formal in its speech, as it tobogganed through the vapors. It said, "Fal-de-ral, fal-de-ral."

Later, I asked the ostrich, "Where is this world I'm supposed to plant my feet on?" But the ostrich had already planted its head in a soft pile of dark.

Then, I asked the rooster, "Where is this world I'm supposed to strut upon?"

The cocky rooster didn't answer.

Instead, all the birds seemed to gather.

For a little while, they did nothing. Then, the emu *boomed* the world. The duck waddled past and *quacked* it. The penguin *fal-de-ral'd* it, and the ostrich *rolly-poled* it with its ball-shaped body and pole-shaped legs, inadvertently inventing the game *Poleball*, which has since been lost to memory.

Can you imagine shaping the world with your voices like that? The ostrich rolled it right under my three feet. I was the first to have three. You can be rightly proud of that.

Ah, yes, the light.

Finally, that puffed-up old rooster opened his beak. He *cock-a-doodle-do'd* the light. That's what he does to this day. I've seen him, oh, have I, with all nine of mine eyes. He struts atop the lost gates to the untamed country. We're on the other side.

I've warned you about mirrors. Here's another warning: Beware of turkeys. With their wattles all a-wagging, they will *gobble-gobble* down what others have shaped up.

Run along now and look for that fence. My eyes have seen better days.

Could somebody help me out of this thing?

THE THREE CRANES

At the edge of a pond, there lived an old crane who was missing a wing and so could only fly in circles. Actually, it couldn't really fly at all but sort of hopped and flapped, hopped and flapped, hopped and flapped to make a circle.

"At least it's not an oval," said the crane with its neck out, "as that would be ridiculous."

Did you know that cranberries got their name from cranes? A crane without an ear named them so. It cut the letter *e* off the word because *e* stands for *ear*. That one could fly quite well. Unfortunately, it could only hear in circles.

"At least I don't hear in ovals," it was heard saying, shortly after naming those little, red berries after itself because of how much it liked to eat them, "as that would be ridiculous."

One day, the story goes, these two old cranes met at a party given in honor of a third, who was missing a leg. The third was expounding on his gladness that he didn't walk in ovals when these two, who were strangers to him, finished his sentence, right up to the period after the word *ridiculous*.

From that moment on, the three cranes were broth-ers—Fly No Oval, Hear No Oval, and Walk No Oval. They tried tangling their long necks together and lifting off the ground as one bird who could fly straight with five wings; they tried the same thing to hear straight with five ears; and again to walk straight with five legs. But each attempt ended abruptly when the long semi-straightness it began with suddenly curved too sharply into Oval. After these failures, the three cranes wouldn't even tangle their necks together

to make a straight stretch of twisted rope for flightless birds
to climb to heaven.

MONUMENT

It was supposed to be a monument to what we'd been. The inscription said so. It also said we were better now, though its lack of specificity left us wondering. If we'd gone backward, the monument praised what it formerly disparaged. Or, was the inscription kept up to date without our knowledge? Changed a tiny dot of a letter at a time.

Clearly we needed a better monument. I brought it up at the meeting. Jan was late and asked me to repeat myself. Then, Dave asked Jan to paraphrase what I'd said, saying his attention had been lost to the bubbles in his belly. We all had bubbles in our bellies. They were made by Mexican Jumping Beans, which we devoured at our meetings. It was part of the decorum. The bubbles hardened like plastic and inside were miniature scenes from the old days in Mexico. The old days were close enough to touch, if it wasn't for the plastic, and this made it difficult to tell the difference between them and the new, which brings us back to the topic at hand, namely, Why Change a Perfectly Good Monument? At least that's how Jan had paraphrased my remarks, and already it was on a banner behind her. She carried the most weight that year, which meant she had the most plastic bubbles inside with scenes from Old Mexico.

Little by little, the monument changed and eventually came to look like a warehouse. We changed too. Back when Jan carried the most weight, I don't think we were cardboard cutouts with fishbowl stomachs full of miniatures for sale.

The Spider King

On a somewhat special island in the deep brown sea, there lived a spider who was made the king—not because he was the biggest or the wisest living thing, for these he was not, nor even because he had a crown of gold around his abdomen, which he did, by chance, but because of his mustache, which was very like a man's. His mustache was so long that it got stuck in any web he tried to make, so he ordered others to make them for him, which wasn't easy for the tortoise, let me tell you, and this ordering about also made him a natural to be the king. Yet, he couldn't get into the webs once they were woven. Whenever he tried, his curling mustache caught like a hook on some strand or other, and he was left stranded, eight legs dangling. Still, he was stubborn and wouldn't think of a trim. His mustache was, after all, what made him king.

His name was Frank.

One day, as Frank was walking regally about the sand, the long hairs of his mustache tripped up a Queen Spider. They caught and dragged her over a rough patch. If you will notice, all patches are rough to something that size. Shortly thereafter, the two fell in love.

Frank waited for the appropriate length of time to say this to her: "I love you very much. Now, please stand under that palm tree until you give me a baby." That's the way such things were done by his kind.

As the Queen Spider had been waiting to be told this, it was easier for her than normal to do what she was told. The king brought her food, though he could have just as well ordered someone else to do it. This, however, was an intimate matter, and all kings before him, as far as he knew, had done the same. The palm tree got its food from wherever it could. It grew, and it grew. Finally, a wind blew, and a baby fell from the tree in a roundish, nuttish ball. It squashed the Queen Spider dead.

"How regrettable," thought the king, "when it happens to you."

Rarely was he this philosophical. It might have been because he was now truly a Black Widower (you can tell one by the gold crown around his abdomen).

Soon enough, that tragic nut of a baby poked out two chubby legs (only two!), got up clumsily and waddled off in a man-babyish way, never to be seen again, though there were reports that the prince had set out to sea.

Frank was left with his mustache. That, and the crater his baby had made. At last, he filled in the crater to bury his bride. Ah, but the king also had his pride, and his kingly belief that things should proceed as he saw fit and not just any way they wished.

He could require Baby Palms to drop something else from on high. He could decree that all queens thereafter must stand a little to one side.

But it was Old Serendipity who found King Frank his solution. The king had been hiding in the Royal Gardens, so as not to be seen as he attempted to spin a web. His mustache didn't get hooked this time, which was good. It was the first clue that something was new. Still, what Frank made was more of a silken bed, really, than a web. It would have seemed a dismal failure to any other spider, but Frank was king, and this was the best work he'd done. The bed was certainly of kingly proportions. It stretched between two Baby Palm trunks and might have caught Mr. Fruit Fly, Mrs. Dragon Fly and their entire extended families, were it not

for something missing in the character of its sticking. This
was sadly disappointing.

Frank lowered himself to the sand and was about to
walk away when a Queen Spider, who'd snuck into the Royal
Gardens, called to him.

"Nothing so *see-able* have I ever seen," said she in
six-eyed admiration of Frank's abomination. She came and
stood directly beneath his unsticky, silken bed.

They fell in love in an instant, which was a good thing
because, before they knew what was happening, a ripe baby
had broken loose from the tree above.

King Frank cried, "Stand to one side!"

Alas, his queen was too frightened. Her eyes could
only stare. But instead of squashing her, the baby went
ham-MUCK, as it was caught in the king's bed.

And when its chubby legs poked out, they went right
through the spaces in Frank's web. Not only was his queen
still alive, but also his baby couldn't waddle off, never to
be seen again.

Frank made more *hammocks*, as they came to be called,
and pretty soon they were all filled with babies. Now, the only
problem was how to get rid of them once they'd grown.

THE ROBOT

No human ever found it, the robot buried in the dirt ten thousand years before by a wild pack of aliens.

The robot's drive to know was gone. Its battery had run down. Still, its memory retained its thoughts, right up to the last garbled fragment. None of these was ever sent home. The robot had not been designed that way.

There had been three main categories of thought for the robot: What is that? Where did it come from? Why is it here? These questions were asked of all variety of matter and conglomerations thereof. Lesser categories included, What am I doing in this dirt?

With each new layer of sediment blown over it, the robot's answers changed. Sometimes, distant answers circled back to previous ones. Other times, they shot further away. The last garbled fragment was an attempt to do both at the same time. It might never be known if the robot succeeded. The wild pack did not record where they buried it. Their less-than-wild descendents had no way of knowing where to look.

GREENER PASTURES

And so the giant, man-eating frog left town for greener pastures—that would be any town he hadn't already devoured, even if it wasn't green, as long as it sprouted a thick mat of luncheon meat, namely human beings.

If you could get to know him, the frog had a good side. His warts, each larger than a carriage full of people, were not the kind you could catch; his breath was sweet; and he liked children.

In the middle of the next town, he sunk into a lake, so his gas would move more quickly through his body. Only his eyes were out of the water, and they didn't like what they saw, which was the lake overflowing and drowning his breakfast.

The amphibian had dreams of being an architect like his father, or, at least, a carpenter who could faithfully carry out his father's master plans. Eating his way through town, the frog-eyed prince studied the churches and shaped his dung heaps into replicas, including the spires.

When he left once more for greener pastures, the people were stuck there, praying for their own.

THE LAST SUPPER

The last supper was long overdue. First supper had been served hours before. Finally, the bread was passed, but there was such talk around it and then the wine that Peter feared this particular last supper might go on forever.

And it did.

Here is how it happened: All were eager to devour the cooked lamb. Yet, his sunken eyes held them off, saying, "Freeze! Yea, just as you are with your leaning in and facing out, your placating and posturing, and your pointing of tongues. Hold it there, oh my brothers, and such a supping as this one shall last and last."

It was a lot for cooked lamb's eyes to say; yet, the painter wouldn't lift his brush until they said just that.

He washed his hands. Though many colors had been used, only red swirled down the basin.

THE FINGER

On a less-than-lucky night in the merry month of M—, the limb of a live oak shivered as the window it had been tapping suddenly broke, and the limb's middle finger went right through.

A woman complained. A man got to his feet. Hands yanked on the limb and snapped off its middle finger.

Skidding beneath the bed, the lost appendage withered and curled. It lay dormant forty-seven years before the now old woman looked down there. The finger beckoned her under and struck like a snake.

THE FATHER

Your face in the mirror becomes two, then three. Hair spreads across them and into the room. It braids itself into your beard, and then pulls you in. You are alone with your face. But you don't recognize it. On the other side, everything is different because it's exactly the same and you don't know it.

Your face in the mirror becomes two, then three. Hair spreads across them and into the room. It braids itself into your beard. The mirror uses this to pull itself off the wall. As it approaches, one face disappears, then another. A single face remains, across from yours. When they touch, the silver glass turns to water, and your noses drop like coins.

Your face in the mirror becomes two, then three. Hair spreads across them and into the room. It braids itself into your beard, which begins to have a mind of its own. The beard detaches itself and walks out the door into daylight. When you turn back to the wall, the mirror is gone. You walk through the wall into night.

The night in your face becomes another beard, a beard from which new things are forever being born. Ants, sand flies, cockroaches, termites, king spiders, hermit crabs. A curly-tail lizard hatches too early. Its thin legs twitch and collapse. A snipe pokes its beak out and snatches the lizard, along with one of your hairs.

The hair falls to earth and sprouts a mustache. The mustache digs roots in the ground. The ground has roots in the cellar. A girl opens her eyes. They blink at him in the dizzying tropical sunlight. The bearded father picks her up by the arm, brushes off fire ants and sand. Seeing the broken lizard eggs, he picks them from her hair.

Friday

BROCCOLI

He was a vegetable scholar. She, an Italian head of broccoli. When he told her the Latin derivation of *broccoli* means *arm*, she sighed, having heard it before.

Misreading her sigh as admiration, the vegetable scholar reached for her body. His hands withdrew immediately, for she was all head. Something he should have known.

She sighed to herself at having never flowered.

Misreading it again, he put a pot to boil.

They waited together, he watching the pot.

He slipped her in without a splash.

She sighed like a lobster.

THE PLATFORM

A man and a woman stepped onto a platform. They didn't know it was moving—at first sideways and then down and then slantways, going up.

The man rubbed his brow ridge and asked for his glove back. The woman said he must have dropped it. On his hands and knees, the man felt around for the glove and decided it had gone off the edge. The woman said she didn't know there was an edge. Now, the man wasn't sure either. Back on his knees, he couldn't find one in any direction. Then, he couldn't find the woman. When at last he bumped into her legs, he clung to them. She allowed this to go on for some time. Then, she freed herself, and, in so doing, she fell off the edge.

HUMPERT

Humpert Dumpert had a great fall. It was only natural because he was a puff of wind and loved the autumn. But Humpert had a problem. He wanted to push a giant egg off a wall, as his friend had done to Humpty Dumpty, but all the kings horses and all the kings men, and Humpty wasn't ever coming back again. There weren't others like him either.

By winter, Humpert Dumpert wished he could stop blowing altogether. Yet, the world kept turning and pulling on his feet.

Then, he remembered Alice, the little girl who'd met Humpty once and had since taken to perching herself on the porch wall of her grandmother's house, rocking back and forth with her knees to her chest. If Humpert could cause some mischief there, he might begin to feel more like a gust.

But when Humpert's blows were fierce enough and in the right direction, the girl was not on the wall. What was worse, she began to sit there less and less, as the years stretched her awkwardly up.

None too early, the wind puff's moment arrived. Alice, now a young woman and rocking like an egg for probably the last time, tipped forward just so, and Humpert Dumpert had his way.

It was not at all like Wonderland.

MISSISSIPPI

Not long ago, there was a nose. It wasn't any *body's* nose; it was its own nose. In fact, no *body* even knew this nose. Or his brother. The two of them were quite alone. Therefore, nobody knows the trouble they'd smelled. Except me, and I will tell you if you have ears enough to hear.

The noses didn't share the same mother. Or father. Actually, they didn't share anything at all with each other, and that, more than anything, is what made them brothers. That, and an unquestionable similarity between the *i*'s. Why, the *i*'s in *Mississippi*, of course. That's where they lived. Not in the river. Or the state. But the word. The first nose made its home between the first and second *i*. The second, between the second and third. A baby brother tagged along between the third and fourth *i*, but he always smelled too much of *p p* to be given any notice.

So, these noses, as I say, had smelled trouble in their day. To the first nose, it smelled like *s*nakes. To the second like *s*ardines. And the trailing odor of their baby brother tinged every scent with *p*.

What's that? You say your name is Earnest? Well, then, there you have it.

JACK AND JILL

Jack and Jill fell into a hole with their pail and couldn't get out. Other couples joined them. Soon, two dozen were in it. Then, two thousand.

The hole became a mound new couples had to climb before falling onto. At the foot of the mound, Jill's well was dry, and the handle on Jack's pump wouldn't work.

Eventually, they remembered they were supposed to go up a hill to fetch the water. But they were stuck, so Jack heaved the pail up the mound. It tumbled down and broke his crown, and then Jill was feeling much better.

CHICKEN OUTFIT

It wasn't Chicken Little but rather the biggest chicken who told the others the sky was falling. She was not so dumb as to believe it herself. It was her way of keeping them from seeing what she was doing, which was robbing the henhouse. You see, the biggest chicken wasn't really a chicken but a wolf in sheep's clothing; only her clothing was a chicken's.

The outfit had belonged to her mother, who'd got it from her mother before her. The hardworking grandmother made it from scratch from the leftover feathers of a year's chicken dinners. The beak was little sheep's bones, pasted together and stained with blood. It had to be stained anew each month, first by the grandmother, then by the mother, and now by the daughter.

A smallish sheep took to following her between the henhouse and the cave. Not recognizing the he-wolf in sheep's clothing, the she-wolf invited him in. Before she could take his sheepskin coat, however, which she meant to do with her canines, he pounced first and ripped a breast off her outfit. Whereupon, a thousand stolen chicks poured out and bowled him over, squeaking, "Papa!"

THE LEFT HAND

The plan was for the forefinger to find an inn near the road where the whole hand could sleep. It was a left hand and had escaped the night before from the oppression of the right. Among other things, the right had refused to acknowledge that the hand was even left-handed, which it had always been. But, apparently, the right was always right, and the left would always be left behind, left out, left with the worst jobs, like wiping the crack and picking the nose, though not without a scrubbing in between, which the right was only too happy to give.

No inn would take the left hand, however, with a ring still on its finger. The ring began to feel like a shackle clamped on it by the right. The thumb tried to work the ring up over the lower knuckle. The hand scraped it against a stone. Desperate, it sawed off its own ring finger on a jagged scrap of tin. The pinkie cowered to see it, while the middle finger swelled.

But then no inn would take the hand for its tell-tale bloody stump.

CHINESE FINGER TRAP

The scattered straw had had enough of the elephant foot's pranks. It wove itself into a large-scale Chinese finger trap and waited, crouching.

The elephant foot must have known because it did not stamp there again.

Instead, an unsuspecting rhinoceros triggered an attack by what seemed to be a leg warmer made of straw that it couldn't shake off.

Realizing what had happened, the straw tried to unweave itself, but it was no use. It had been caught in its own trap. The rhinoceros fared better. Its leg warmer incited the admiration of many females who offered their rumps. Though the trait was never passed on, the females kept trying for it, braiding their hind legs with his.

HAT AND RACK

The man may have mistaken his wife for a hat, but the woman mistook her husband for a hat rack. He wasn't sure why the hat liked to hang coats on him. She couldn't answer why the hat rack tried to put her on its crown. When they went to bed, she felt he was all arms. He felt she was distinctly out of place. The few times he submitted to wearing her there, his head swam. Out to dinner, she thought him rigid, while he worried she was liable to sit on any head. Back home, she hung her wet umbrella on him, and he threw her in the closet.

WATER BALLET

"Useless. Godforsaken lumps of dough." He was speaking of the former ballerina's breasts. He kneaded them once more and gave up. Without the requisite cocktail of hormones, he didn't see the point of shifting them around or teasing their collapsed nipples.

Outside, a spider was caught in melted ice cream. Though its limbs had given up, it went on living.

He washed spider and ice cream away with his piss.

Gathering in a pool, his piss used the spider's now upturned legs to do something it had always dreamed of—water ballet.

THE SEA SQUIRT

Once, in the shallow, green sea, right next to a large, dozing crab, a baby sea squirt uncurled the spinelike tail that made it a distant cousin to man—too distant to be invited to even the largest weddings—and set about finding a home.

Lick! Splick! went its tail, propelling its unusual head through the water. Instead of a hat or even hair, this cousin of man wears a sucker on its head; at least it does in its youth. Once the sucker attaches to a home, the head becomes more of a foot, and the squirt transforms into something like a human heart. It pumps water in through one valve and squirts it out through another.

The little squirt swam along until it met a dock piling, which it asked about the severity of surges in the neighborhood. It spoke by spitting water with its sucker. Disappointingly, the sound wasn't big enough for the dock piling to hear.

The squirt went on to find a boat hull sticking down into the waves, which it asked about the quality of debris in the area from dead plants and animals. Unlike its distant cousin, once a sea squirt attaches to a home, it remains fixed there for the rest of its life. All its suppers must then arrive at its doorstep, or it will starve. The boat hull didn't say anything either, unless you counted the senseless slappings of water against it, which went on and on.

Tiring of its larval stage, a stage in which it was free-roaming but couldn't really squirt up to its name, the creature resorted to asking the dozing crab about its neighborhood in the shallow, green sea. The water spat by the squirt's tiny sucker nudged the crab's left eyestalk just so.

"Can't you see I'm sleeping?" the crustacean said irritably.

"Well," thought the squirt, "if it can afford to sleep so much as that, this must be a very rich neighborhood indeed." And so the sea squirt attached itself at once to the top of the crab's shell by means of the clever sucker on its head, which was proving far more useful than even a broad-brimmed hat. After resorbing its tail, the squirt became a lovely pumping heart of sorts, just behind the crab's eyestalks and out of reach of its claw.

Now, this was the life! Immobile on a mobile home with all its suppers brought to it on a platter of silver water. And it had both male and female reproductive parts, which made it feel less alone. Or, was that more alone? The squirt could never quite tell. It wasn't like it would mate with itself. That would be worse than marrying your cousin. So, probably, it felt more alone, which meant it was time to fertilize some eggs. Or else shed some.

"Git along, little doggie," said the jet of water the squirt could now blast out its valve. It blew the crab's eyestalks forward and tossed them all about.

An interesting fact about a squirt's way of speaking is that its bodily waste shoots out with the water.

"Do you mind!" stammered the crab in an orchestra of dirty bubbles.

Those bubbles felt good on all the squirt's parts, so it blasted the crab's eyestalks again and shivered in pleasure among the bubbles stammered back.

"This could almost do just fine," thought the maturing squirt, shedding eggs for the very first time.

Unfortunately, the eggs floated straight into the mouth of its home.

Thinking quickly for one who'd recently sucked up its own nervous system, the squirt shot the crab's eyestalks again. The crab talked dirty in return and even scuttled and bucked to try to get the squirt off, which it did (in another sense of the phrase), for the bubbles and the bucking made the squirt release its first seeds. These too found their way into the crab's mouth, where they fertilized the eggs already there.

Weeks later, the dozen larval squirts who'd managed to stay alive by burrowing into the crab's soft cheeks came flagellating out its mouth, their tiny, malformed heads covered in hair.

Saturday

THE CLINIC

A long time ago in a galaxy far away, two things happened that don't concern us. Though the repercussions were felt far and wide, they weren't felt here, and this is where we are, on the fifth rock from our dying son, who was cast so many rocks away for misbehaving. Plus, they have the best hospitals there, each with a mossy green side for taking fresh air and exercise.

Now, on Saturday next we're all going to visit him and his sister. She's one rock over at the Clinic for Breathing While Holding Your Head Underwater. It can only be achieved by the most mentally unstable, and even they need help. As we're born with gills these days, one would think it shouldn't take a special mind or schooling to make them work. Alas, perhaps one day that will not be the case. Sooner rather than later, I hope, as the water is now up to my exit hole.

"What about you, Stan? How's the water at your house? And how's your daughter coming along at the Clinic? Swimmingly? I thought so. I could never tell what that girl was thinking."

THE HAIR

There once was an island all covered in hair, except for a bald spot of sand on top of a hill. Because of what happened there, the hair will never grow back.

The hair liked to make nests of itself of various sizes and weaves. It used these to coax birds out of the sky. Once it had a bird, it strangled and stuffed it full of itself. Quite a collection of stuffed birds were on display on that island, their feet bound to the twigs and branches of the hair's fake bushes. Those were the decoys.

When the wind was just right, the hair made throatlike tunnels of itself and imitated birdcalls.

"WHIP-poor-WILL… WHIP-poor-WILL," chirped the hair at twilight, sometimes four hundred times without stopping. And down came a female whippoorwill to take a turn whipping Will. Soon enough she discovered the lash she was using had somehow gotten around her neck and was beginning to tighten.

"Chuck-WILL'S-Widow… Chuck-WILL'S-Widow," the hair twittered before dawn, sometimes eight hundred times without stopping. Down came a male chuck-will's-widow to take Will's widow for his wife. But it was he who was taken.

This is what happened on the hill:

The hair made a lovely nest. It attracted a lovely bird. The hair squeezed the bird to death but not before three eggs popped out. It tried to strangle the eggs but only managed to incubate them.

By the time the eggs hatched, the hair had grown over them and, because of this, too used to them. The baby birds ate their way out, which gave the hair such a nasty cut that it never grew back.

THE ROPE

A man opened his barn door and discovered that it no longer led to his barn. It led to his neighbor's barn, which was identical to his, except it had termites and no cows.

He shut the door and opened it again.

On the way to his neighbor's farm, he wondered if he could have got there sooner by just stepping into the barn and then coming out again on his neighbor's property.

He found his neighbor in the barn, gripping a rope with both hands. The rope was tied to a ring in the ground that looked like a cow's nose ring. Together, they pulled until all the man's cows had come out of the ground and taken their proper place in his barn.

But the barn was still on his neighbor's property. So, he pulled once more until his land came out of his neighbor's. It buried his neighbor and his neighbor's land, though it didn't bury the cows, who had enough sense to step up.

Not long after, the bewildered man tried to hang himself from a beam with the rope but only fell through the ground to where his wife was pulling the other end.

NICKY

They couldn't find any of them in the house. Nicky's crayons were on the table along with drawings of himself, his mother, and his father in all the seasons. In spring, trees sprouted so densely, they forced Nicky's parents out of the picture. Summer showed the family together in the attic window, while a gray bird on the rooftop sang what they sang, only better. In autumn, they touched mittens atop a pile of yellow leaves. Winter showed a snow fort like the one Nicky's father had built. Their bodies had parts inside and parts outside the fort, and a coal-smudged snowman stood nearby. The snowman had broken-off tree limbs for arms. It was these Nicky used to take his parents from their bed.

THE CHAIR

The red plastic chair had always been sure it was not meant to be sat on. That's why it had its bottom to the world when the blizzard came. Afterward, only the feet were visible, each capped by a slender column of fluff. The chair might have shaken the snow off but didn't want to draw more attention to itself. Already, the girl inside was donning her mittens; the dog was pawing the glass; and the man with the mustache was writing something down.

THE TROUT

Beneath the dried-out apple of the sun, a man grown old from searching streams died upon brown twigs and leaves.

Once, on his carpeted floor, a glimmering girl with blossoms in her hair became a trout. He should never have turned his back to keep the fire going.

The fish gasped until he pierced it with a switch of hazel he used for fishing.

Yet, no matter how he tried, he could find no girl inside.

Nor in any other fish in all his years of looking.

THE SINGING

She sang in a language we did not understand, though it was beautiful to all.

In the morning, when the sun went down, The Singing brought us groggy from our holes and into formations, where we could be counted and given bread.

By midday, as we sopped up gravy from seawater, it gave us stamina and hope.

At dusk, in our exhaustion, as the half-light of dawn pried us open, The Singing closed our eyes.

Then, my own voice tried to sing a different meaning to my life. I only grew confused because The Singing was there too, pulling the melody off key.

We might have wished for silence, but that would be worse. Silence was a circling vulture, screeching too plainly, "Three pounds of flax!"

6 x 6

A basement room with a single, small window. Outside, something green, attractive to wasps. Its leaves told me when it was spring, summer, or fall and what the air was doing. The naked sprig, the other things.

A vent near the ceiling brought warm air and voices. Only cats and squirrels passed by the window, so, for the longest time, I thought the voices came from something like them—Queen Squirrels so gigantic they could no longer move. And those little, agitated ones outside were her Workers. And I had been grown for them in this live-food storage cell.

With my feet pressed against any wall, the crown of my head touched the one opposite. Standing, it brushed the low ceiling. They didn't walk upright. Such things were good signs I was being held against my will.

Sometimes the room was lifted up. This was preceded by a sudden change of darkness in the window, as if a blanket had been thrown over it. When the movement was steady, I couldn't tell I was moving, until the room was snapped back into place and the blanket removed.

A smaller vent dropped food pellets, shaped like hamburgers. Excrement went through the flooring and was collected while I slept.

Sleep came in tides. I never saw a moon but could feel the effects.

I folded my spindly arms, having no idea how I knew what I knew.

THIS MORTAL COIL

Even had it wished to, the metal spring could not very well shuffle off, as the great playwright seemed to be advising it to do through the voice of his character. The spring was done with and, unless Shakespeare himself or some other of his company wanted to press it down again under a folio or two, it had no tension left to move, much less to shuffle, which might have been beyond its abilities anyway.

Then, Hamlet kicked the spring, while fretting over his lines. A few tumbles and it wound up on its side, rolling toward the pit. It couldn't help falling in. Fortunately, the spring landed squarely on its end.

It was leaping again!

The subsequent rounds of tension and release, as this particular mortal coil crouched and sprang, played skillfully on the nerves of almost all at rehearsal, making Polonius, in particular, believe they were really onto something. As for the playwright, he was after something else.

THE AUTHOR

I talk to myself. I fiddle continually with my nose, pinching the end of it, bending it to the side. I read random pages of books, from folk tales to physics, and rearrange them on shelves. I pick a subject like termites and research it on the web for a phrase, a habit, a trait, like the heads of soldiers being large enough to block passages against intruders.

Yesterday, a framed photograph of my great uncle standing before a barn spoke this line: "A man opened his barn door and discovered that it no longer led to his barn." Another time it was my daughter's miniature, plastic giraffe. Holding it close for several minutes, I thought: "She was a giraffe of modest proportions, except for her spots, which threatened to overtake her. Her white socks had escaped the spots by threatening, in turn, to pull themselves up." Before bed last night, I placed the current *New York Times Magazine* under my wife's side of the mattress, opened to a full-page photograph of an elephant's foot.

I dreamt of lion's-head knockers loping through the neighborhood, ringing people's bells.

Then, in the morning, the straw around the elephant's foot wove itself into a Chinese finger trap to catch the foot, but the elephant never stepped there again.

In conversation, my ears get distracted by the smallest noises, which become larger, until my ears look like a clown's, and I've lost all interest in what the other person is saying. Or, the tree in the window waves the curved and forked limb it has been growing toward me for decades. Or, a boulder in the yard will sit with such intensity, like a steaming bull or a native chief, that I have to know what it's doing and why it is there.

My wife leaves the mayonnaise jar open, or eggs boiling on the burner, or clothes in the washer, or a suitcase half unpacked, or toys on the stair, or books on the floor, or milk curdled in a cup, or a lump of cheese on the counter, or yesterday's oatmeal stuck to a bowl, or the stereo on, or a car window down, or the garage door open, or the thermostat all the way up, or gas filling the oven, or the bathtub running—and again I am a killer.

THE OTHER HALF

"I want to see how the other half live," an ambitious young wall mirror said.

In the succeeding years, it looked most everywhere it could, but whichever way it faced, it could not see backward through its own face.

Eventually, the less-than-young mirror got its wish. It grew eyes in the back of its head. That is, another mirror was hung across the hall.

"I had no idea," said the mirror on reflection.

The other said nothing.

>€

ACKNOWLEDGMENTS

Thanks to the editors of the publications in which the following stories first appeared:

Beacons: "Still Life with Painter," "The Sound";
Boulevard: "The Sea Squirt," "Three Wise Men";
Caketrain: "Chinese Finger Trap," "New Heaven," "The Hermit Crab," "The Other Half";
Conjunctions: "6 x 6," "Almost Borges," "Counter-Puncher";
Double Room: "No Place to Crawl," "The Ever After," "The Hair";
elimae: "Broccoli," "The Last Supper";
Fiction: "The Wife";
The Greensboro Review: a version of "Newshound," titled "The Only News Worth Reporting";
Sentence: "The Log," "The Yarn".

ABOUT THE AUTHOR

Daniel Grandbois's writing has appeared in *Conjunctions*, *Fiction*, *Boulevard*, *Sentence*, *Del Sol Review*, and the anthologies *Freak Lightning* and *Online Writing: The Best of the First Ten Years*, among others. His second book, *The Hermaphrodite (An Hallucinated Memoir)*, with forty original woodcuts by Argentine printmaker Alfredo Benavidez Bedoya, is forthcoming from Green Integer in fall 2008. Also a musician, Grandbois plays or has played in three of the pioneering bands of "The Denver Sound": Slim Cessna's Auto Club, Tarantella, and Munly.

BOA Editions, Ltd.
American Reader Series

No. 1   *Christmas at the Four Corners of the Earth*
Prose by Blaise Cendrars
Translated by Bertrand Mathieu

No. 2   *Pig Notes & Dumb Music: Prose on Poetry*
By William Heyen

No. 3   *After-Images: Autobiographical Sketches*
By W. D. Snodgrass

No. 4   *Walking Light: Memoirs and Essays on Poetry*
By Stephen Dunn

No. 5   *To Sound Like Yourself: Essays on Poetry*
By W. D. Snodgrass

No. 6   *You Alone Are Real to Me: Remembering Rainer Maria Rilke*
By Lou Andreas-Salomé

No. 7   *Breaking the Alabaster Jar: Conversations with Li-Young Lee*
Edited by Earl G. Ingersoll

No. 8   *I Carry A Hammer In My Pocket For Occasions Such As These*
By Anthony Tognazzini

No. 9   *Unlucky Lucky Days*
By Daniel Grandbois

Colophon

Unlucky Lucky Days, stories by Daniel Grandbois, is set in Adobe Garamond, a digital font designed in 1989 by Robert Slimbach (1956–) based on the French Renaissance roman types of Claude Garamond (ca. 1480–1561) and the italics of Robert Granjon (1513–1589).

The publication of this book is made possible, in part, by the special support of the following individuals:

Anonymous (2)
Alan & Nancy Cameros
Gwen & Gary Conners
Peter & Karen Conners
Peter & Sue Durant
Pete & Bev French
Judy & Dane Gordon
Alan & Dorothy Grandbois
Kip & Debby Hale
Peter & Robin Hursh
Willy & Bob Hursh
X. J. & Dorothy M. Kennedy
Archie & Pat Kutz
Rosemary & Lewis Lloyd
Boo Poulin
Steven O. Russell & Phyllis Rifkin-Russell
Vicki & Richard Schwartz
Joseph Shields & Patti Hall
Jerry Vorrasi
Lee & Rob Ward
Patricia D. Ward-Baker
Pat & Mike Wilder
Glenn & Helen William